RICH

A DYAMONDE DANIEL Book

Also by Nikki Grimes

Jazmin's Notebook

Bronx Masquerade

The Road to Paris

Make Way for Dyamonde Daniel

RICH

A DYAMONDE DANIEL Book

Nikki Grimes

illustrated by
R. Gregory Christie

G. P. Putnam's Sons
Penguin Young Readers Group

G. P. PUTNAM'S SONS
A division of Penguin Young Readers Group.
Published by The Penguin Group.
Penguin Group (USA) Inc., 375 Hudson Street, New York, NY 10014, U.S.A.
Penguin Group (Canada), 90 Eglinton Avenue East, Suite 700, Toronto, Ontario
M4P 2Y3, Canada (a division of Pearson Penguin Canada Inc.).
Penguin Books Ltd, 80 Strand, London WC2R 0RL, England.
Penguin Ireland, 25 St. Stephen's Green, Dublin 2, Ireland
(a division of Penguin Books Ltd.).
Penguin Group (Australia), 250 Camberwell Road, Camberwell, Victoria 3124,
Australia (a division of Pearson Australia Group Pty Ltd).
Penguin Books India Pvt Ltd, 11 Community Centre, Panchsheel Park,
New Delhi - 110 017, India.
Penguin Group (NZ), 67 Apollo Drive, Rosedale, North Shore 0632,
New Zealand (a division of Pearson New Zealand Ltd).
Penguin Books (South Africa) (Pty) Ltd, 24 Sturdee Avenue, Rosebank,
Johannesburg 2196, South Africa.
Penguin Books Ltd, Registered Offices: 80 Strand, London WC2R 0RL, England.

Library of Congress Cataloging-in-Publication Data
Grimes, Nikki.   Rich : a Dyamonde Daniel book / Nikki Grimes ;
illustrated by R. Gregory Christie.   p. cm.
Summary: Free is excited about a local poetry contest because of its cash prize,
but when he and Dyamonde befriend a classmate that is homeless and living in
a shelter, they rethink what it means to be rich or poor.
[1. Homelessness—Fiction. 2. Friendship—Fiction. 3. Poetry—Fiction.
4. African Americans—Fiction.] I. Christie, Gregory, 1971– ill. II. Title.
PZ7.G88429Ri 2009   [Fic]—dc22   2009001033

ISBN 978-0-399-25176-4

For Ariana Katherine—N.G.

To Jerry Gant,
artist and poet extraordinaire—R.G.C.

Contents

Here comes the
fabulous Dyamonde Daniel
and her best friend, Free—
and that means there's going
to be an adventure!

The World of Dyamonde Daniel

Dyamonde Daniel

Dyamonde Daniel is a third-grader who likes to know everything that's going on. She gives terrific advice, she's great at math and she has her friend Free all figured out. She loves meeting people and knows that being "rich" doesn't always mean having a lot of money.

Free

He's Dyamonde's best friend, and he dreams of being able to buy all the video games he wants. And winning a poetry contest with a cash prize would be a great start! Free thinks that should be easy since he knows he's a great poet.

Damaris Dancer

Damaris is the quiet girl in class who never raises her hand for anything. She runs away from Dyamonde when Dyamonde sees her in their neighborhood. Does Damaris have a secret? Dyamonde plans to find out!

Dyamonde's mom

Dyamonde lives with her mom in an apartment, and they are super close. Mrs. Daniel is nice and makes the most awesome pancakes on Saturday mornings.

Rich

Dyamonde and Free stood in front of a store window.

"I hate being poor," said Free. "Ever since my dad lost his job, all my mom seems to say is 'We can't afford this, we can't afford that.'"

Dyamonde Daniel would not trade Free for anything. He was

her best friend, wasn't he? But that boy had a lot to learn.

"First off," said Dyamonde, "I've seen you buy lots of things. And second, you are not poor."

"Then how come I can't buy that new video game?"

"My mom says everybody wants something they can't have," said Dyamonde. "That don't—doesn't make you poor."

"Well, what do you call it, then?"

"Not having money right now," said Dyamonde.

"Same thing," grumbled Free.

"No, it isn't," said Dyamonde. "Poor is . . ." Dyamonde thought for a moment. "Poor is having no clothes, and no food, and no place to live, and nobody who cares."

"I guess," said Free. "But I still wish I could get that new video game."

"Well then," said Dyamonde, "you'd better get to school so you can graduate, so you can get a job, so you can buy your *own* video game."

"Forget it, then," said Free.

Dyamonde play-punched him in the arm.

"You call that a punch? You punch like a girl," said Free.

Dyamonde pulled her arm back and punched him for real this time.

"Ouch! I was just kidding!"

"Come on, then," said Dyamonde. "And hurry. Mrs. Cordell said she'd have a surprise for us today."

Surprise

"Attention, class!" said Mrs. Cordell. "I have an announcement."

Great! thought Dyamonde. *Here it comes!*

"First, how many of you like contests?"

Everybody's hand went up except for Dyamonde's. She wanted

to wait and see what this was all about first.

"Well, the local library is sponsoring a poetry contest!" said Mrs. Cordell.

Tameeka groaned. So did Charlie. But then, Charlie groaned about everything.

Mrs. Cordell ignored the groaning.

"The top three poems will be published on the Kids' Page of the Sunday newspaper."

"Oooh!" said one kid.

"I could be famous!" said a second kid.

"You wish!" said a third.

"And the winner," said Mrs. Cordell, "will receive a check for one hundred dollars!"

"Oh, snap!" said Free.

Dyamonde did not even have to look at Free to know that his eyes were bugging out. She could just see him with imaginary dollar signs and little video games floating in front of him.

"Now, who would like an entry form?" asked the teacher.

Free's hand shot up higher than anyone else's. Dyamonde didn't raise hers. She decided to wait for a math contest. That's what she was best at. But she was curious to know who *was* trying out for the contest.

Dyamonde looked around the room and saw lots of hands. One of them belonged to a quiet girl named Damaris Dancer.

Damaris was a pretty girl, really tall, with skin like dark chocolate mixed with strawberries. Her reddish brown hair hung in heavy twists that made Dyamonde think of a lion's mane.

Damaris raised her hand a little higher, just in case Mrs. Cordell hadn't noticed her.

That's strange, thought Dyamonde. *She never raises her hand for anything. I wonder—*

"Psst," said Charlie from the seat next to Dyamonde.

Dyamonde turned to him, annoyed. *Don't psst me,* thought Dyamonde. She would have said as much out loud if Charlie hadn't distracted her by pressing a note in her hand.

Dyamonde unfolded the torn loose-leaf page and read:

I'm a poet
and I know it,
and now I got
the chance to show it.
                    Free

Oh, puleeze! thought Dya-monde, shaking her head. Then she wrote something on the bottom of the page and sent it back.

Can't wait for lunch.
Hope we have punch.
                    Dyamonde

Free laughed and Charlie asked, "What's it say?"—loud.

"Is there something you boys would like to share with the class?" asked Mrs. Cordell.

"No," said Free. "Sorry."

Dyamonde bowed her head to hide her smile.

Lunch Punch

Dyamonde beat Free through the lunch line. She'd downed half a carton of milk by the time he joined her at the table.

"Doesn't look like punch to me," said Free.

"Hardy-har-har," said Dyamonde. "Like your poem was so much better."

"You watch!" said Free. "I'm gonna win that thing."

"Yeah, sure," said Dyamonde. Just then, she noticed Damaris sitting two tables away. She wasn't eating, though. Instead, she was reading a book.

She does that a lot, thought Dyamonde. *In fact, I hardly ever see her eat. Is she on a special diet or something?*

"Hello?" said Free. "Earth to Dy. Is anybody listening?"

"Huh? Sorry," said Dyamonde. "Do you know anything about her?"

"About who?" asked Free.

"Damaris Dancer," said Dyamonde.

"Nope," said Free. "Why?"

"Just wondering," said Dyamonde. "You know, she signed up for the contest. She might be good at writing poems. Her name kinda sounds like poetry."

"So what?" said Free. "Nobody's gonna win that contest except for me. There, you see? I know my poetry."

"Oh, puleeze!" said Dyamonde. "Stop rhyming or—"

"Or you'll walk on out the

door, and you won't come back no more?"

"Quit it!"

"*Any*more, I should have said. Rhyming's messing with my head."

Enough already, thought Dyamonde. "Reed Freeman, stop rhyming right now, or after school, I'll go on a treasure hunt with somebody else."

"Treasure hunt?" That got Free's attention. "What treasure hunt?"

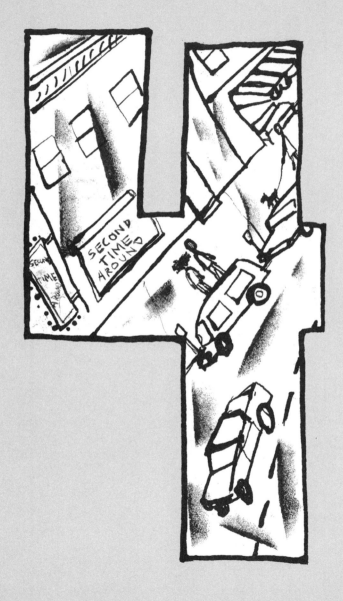

Treasure Hunt

Free loved digging up secrets. Once, he helped his dad dig up an ancient time capsule with records from the olden days that his dad had planted back when he was in high school. Then there was the scavenger hunt Free went on at summer camp. That was fun. He'd never heard of a girl digging up treasure, but if any girl could, it would be Dyamonde.

After school that day, they met out front and headed across the avenue, walking toward Broadway. On Broadway, Dyamonde turned right.

"Where're we going?" asked Free.

"Almost there," said Dyamonde.

Halfway down the block, Dyamonde stopped in front of an old store with a sign that read:

SECOND TIME AROUND

Free froze. He hated secondhand stores.

"I thought we were going to look for treasure," said Free.

"We are," said Dyamonde. "In there. Come on."

Before Free could argue, Dyamonde grabbed his hand and pulled him inside. He held on to the door like his life depended on it and looked up and down the street. He'd die if anybody he knew saw him entering that stinky old place.

Second Time Around wasn't actually stinky, but Free had made up his mind that all secondhand stores were. Not that he was an expert. This was only the third time he'd ever been in one. The other two times, his mom had dragged him into one to shop for clothes. Even the memory made Free say yuck!

Once inside, Dyamonde let Free's hand go.

"What kind of treasure are we supposed to find in here?" asked Free.

"You're kidding, right?" said Dyamonde. "Look around."

"I'm sorry," said Free. "But I don't like these places."

"Why?"

" 'Cause they're full of old clothes and stuff people threw away. Why would I want stuff other people threw away when I could buy something new?"

Dyamonde shook her head impatiently.

"First of all, new is okay, but new is boring. It hasn't been anywhere. And second, how do you know these things were thrown away? Maybe they were left overafter a fire, or maybe a family all of a sudden disappeared, and their perfectly good clothes and furniture and stuff were mysteriously left behind."

"Huh?"

"When I look at the stuff here, I always wonder where it's been, what adventures it's been on. Like those boots. Did somebody wear them to climb a mountain? Or that jacket. Maybe the sleeves of it once blew in the breeze along some famous river, like the Nile. You never know, right?"

Free scratched his head. "I guess," he said.

"It's not just old stuff, Free," said Dyamonde. "Everything has a story. That's kind of what makes it a treasure."

Free nodded, trying to see things Dyamonde's way, trying to understand.

"I'm gonna take a look around," said Dyamonde. "I'll meet you back up here in a few minutes."

"Okay," said Free.

At first, Free just followed Dyamonde with his eyes, watching her slowly make her way down an aisle of old clothes, stopping now and then to feel the fabric or to try on a sweater or a jacket in front of a mirror. Then he began wandering the aisles himself, choosing the one with old books and toys.

The books didn't look half bad, and even the toys looked okay, though they were mostly for little kids. Balls and dolls and whatnot. But there were table games too, like Monopoly. Only he already had a Monopoly set at home.

Free sighed. *I knew it,* he thought. *There are no treasures here.*

Of course, that's when he saw it. A glass jar filled with the most amazing marbles he'd ever seen. It was a small jar, but it must've had twenty marbles in it, at least.

Free reached for the jar, pulled it down gingerly and searched for the price sticker.

Fifty cents! He couldn't believe his eyes.

Free clutched the jar and went to find his friend.

"Look!" said Free, coming up behind Dyamonde. She was studying a small wooden box she'd found on a shelf. Dyamonde turned around to see what Free was so excited about.

"Marbles!" he said. "Aren't they great? Only I can't figure out why anyone would throw good marbles away."

"Maybe they didn't," said Dyamonde. "Maybe there's a story behind it."

"Yeah," said Free. "There must be."

Dyamonde smiled. She was trying real hard not to say I told you so. "How much?"

"Fifty cents! Can you believe it?"

"Great," said Dyamonde. "And here's my treasure for the day—a box for my rock collection." She held up the box, even opened it so he could smell inside.

"Smells good. What is it?"

"Cedar. It's a special kind of wood."

The box was worn in places, but it had a pretty gold latch.

"I'm gonna paint it," said Dyamonde. "Red, of course. Then, it'll be perfect."

"Cool," said Free, who couldn't stop grinning. "I wonder what other great stuff they've got in here. This place is amazing!"

"But I thought you didn't like 'these places,'" said Dyamonde, throwing Free's own words back at him.

"Well, that was before," said Free. "Anyways, why are we standing here *talking*? We're supposed to be *hunting*."

"Go on, then," said Dyamonde. "Nobody's stopping you."

Free zoomed back to the toy aisle while Dyamonde turned her attention to clothes.

Dyamonde had a funny way of shopping for clothes. She didn't pay attention to size or style at first. Instead, she picked her way through the rack looking for the color red. Once she found something in that color, only then would she consider the style. Size was the last thing on her mind. If the piece was too small, that was one thing. But if it was a little too big, Dyamonde figured all she had to do was put a belt on it, right?

Row by row, Dyamonde made her way through the clothes section.

"Oh, well," sighed Dyamonde

after an unsuccessful hunt. "Maybe next time."

Dyamonde went in search of Free. She found him in the book corner, flipping through a copy of *The Way Things Work.*

"Hey," said Dyamonde.

"Hay is for horses," said Free.

Dyamonde ignored that. "Come on. We've gotta go now or we'll never get our homework done tonight."

Free looked up at the clock and realized they'd been in the store for almost an hour. He and Dyamonde took their goodies to the register and paid. Both treasures were small enough to stuff in their backpacks.

"See you next week!" Dyamonde said to the cashier.

"Yeah," added Free. "See you next week!"

As they left the store, Dyamonde thought she saw Damaris entering a building down the street.

"Damaris!" called Dyamonde.

"Where?" asked Free.

"There!" said Dyamonde, pointing. But the girl had already disappeared without ever turning around. Dyamonde shrugged.

"Guess it wasn't her," said Dyamonde. "Sure looked like her, though." *Same lion's mane and everything,* thought Dyamonde. *Oh, well.*

Secrets

One Saturday, Mrs. Daniel joined Dyamonde on a treasure hunt. Only her mom didn't call it that. She called it "shopping."

Moms just have no imagination, thought Dyamonde.

Anyway, when they left Second Time Around, Dyamonde spotted Damaris Dancer exiting a white building down the street. This time, Dyamonde was sure it was the girl from her class.

"Damaris," called Dyamonde.

At first the girl didn't turn around.

"Hey, Damaris! It's me!" said Dyamonde. This time, Damaris looked around. When she saw Dyamonde, she ran in the opposite direction.

That's weird, thought Dyamonde.

"Someone you know?" asked Mrs. Daniel.

"Kind of," said Dyamonde. She

didn't say anything else, and her mom didn't ask more questions.

As they passed the white building, though, Dyamonde noticed the sign above the entrance. It read **SHELTER**.

Dyamonde knew what a shelter was. It was where people went to live when they didn't have anyplace else. She knew that the people who lived in shelters were poor. And now she knew that one of those people was Damaris.

Damaris

The following Monday, Dyamonde caught up with Damaris in the school hall.

"Hey," said Dyamonde. "Why'd you run away from me the other day?"

"Huh?"

"Saturday. Me and my mom were coming out of Second Time

Around, and I saw you coming out of the shelter."

Damaris looked around, nervously twisting a strand of hair. "No, I don't think so," she said.

"Yes. I know it was you. You even turned around when I called your name. But then you ran away."

Damaris glanced up and down the hall to make sure no one else was close enough to hear.

"Look," she said in a whispery voice. "Nobody knows where I live, so please don't tell them. Please!"

"Don't worry," Dyamonde whispered back. "It'll be our secret." Then she closed her mouth with an invisible zipper. After that, Damaris stopped looking so scared.

Damaris avoided Dyamonde for the rest of that day, but on Tuesday, Dyamonde found her in the lunchroom with her usual pile of books and no food in sight. Dyamonde sat down next to her without asking. Free was out sick, so it's not like he would miss her.

"Want some chicken nuggets?" said Dyamonde. "They're extra.

Mom made me this cucumber and avocado sandwich, which I have to eat first."

Damaris glanced at the chicken nuggets and licked her lips.

"I'm not hungry," she said, looking back at her book.

"You sure?" asked Dyamonde. "I really need some help with these nuggets. Mom says it's a sin and a shame to throw food away."

"Well," said Damaris. "Maybe just one."

Dyamonde pushed the plate of chicken toward her, smiling.

Damaris went from being a

reader to being a magician. She made those chicken nuggets disappear in no time flat.

Damaris belched. "Sorry."

"S'okay," said Dyamonde. She burped too, just so Damaris wouldn't feel bad.

Once they were done with lunch, Dyamonde locked arms with Damaris and practically pulled her out to the school yard for recess. Dyamonde liked to know everything, and she'd made up her mind that she was going to get to know Damaris Dancer.

Poetry Contest

"So, you signed up for the poetry contest," Dyamonde said to Damaris.

"Uh-huh. Didn't you?"

Dyamonde shook her head. "I'm not very good at poetry."

"I love it. I write poems all the time," said Damaris. "I'd do the

51

contest even if there wasn't any money to win."

"Really?" From the way the girl's face lit up, Dyamonde believed her.

"I've got a bunch of poems already. Want to see?" said Damaris. She pulled out her notebook before Dyamonde could even answer. The book was filled with page after page of poems. There were hardly any blank pages left.

"Wow," said Dyamonde.

As Dyamonde read her poems, Damaris did something funny

with her face. The corners of her mouth turned up, and the top row of her teeth appeared. Damaris was smiling! Dyamonde had never seen her do that before.

"What are you going to write about for the contest?" asked Dyamonde.

Damaris shrugged. "I have abso-tively, posi-lutely no idea."

"Huh?"

"Absolutely, positively," said Damaris. "I just switched the words around a little. I like to play with words. That's what poetry is, anyway. Playing with words."

"If you say so," said Dyamonde, scratching her head.

"Anyway," said Damaris, "the contest only gives you three topics to choose from, so I'll have to pick one."

"What are they?"

Damaris counted them off on her fingers. "Nature. Make-believe. And home." She whispered the last word, like it was extra-special.

"You should write about home," said Dyamonde.

"How can I? It's not like my family has one, remember?"

"Yeah, but you could write about where you live now."

"What? Write about living in a shelter so people could laugh at me? No, thank you."

"No!" said Dyamonde. "Look: where you live is different from where everybody else lives, so your poem would be different too. And everybody knows it's good to be different in a contest." Dyamonde was absolutely sure she was right. Wasn't she always?

Damaris shut her poetry note-book and put it away. Her smile was gone now.

"You promised you wouldn't tell anybody where I live," whispered Damaris.

"I didn't!" said Dyamonde.

"You promised!" said Damaris. "Now you want me to write about it so everybody will know? Forget it!" Damaris stomped off. Dyamonde ran after her.

"What did I do?" asked Dyamonde.

"Quit following me!" Damaris snapped.

"I just wanted to say I'm sorry for making you so mad."

"Fine," said Damaris. But she still looked pretty mad to Dyamonde.

Dyamonde jumped in front of Damaris to keep her from running away.

"My mom says people laugh at other people 'cause they don't know better," said Dyamonde. "Maybe if they knew what it was like to live in a shelter, they wouldn't laugh. You could be the one to tell them," said Dyamonde. "In a poem."

Damaris listened. Her angry face melted away.

"I don't know," said Damaris. "Maybe."

Both girls were quiet for a moment. They sat down on a bench and turned their faces up to the sun, closing their eyes.

"How come you live in a shelter, anyway?" asked Dyamonde.

With her eyes still closed, Damaris sighed. "My mom was working two jobs and she lost one of 'em. She got late on the rent, so they threw our stuff on the sidewalk and said we had to

go. Mom found another job, but it was too late. Now me and my two brothers and my mom have to stay in a shelter till we can save up enough to get a new apartment."

"Man," said Dyamonde.

"Yeah," said Damaris.

"So what happened to all your stuff?" asked Dyamonde.

Damaris shrugged. "Most of it ended up in some secondhand store, somewhere."

Dyamonde thought of Second Time Around. She thought of all the stories she used to make up in her mind about the clothes, toys and furniture she found there. But this wasn't a made-up story. This was real.

The bell rang, and both girls walked back to class in silence. At the door of their classroom, Dyamonde turned to Damaris.

"I still think you should write about it," she said. "You told me the whole story. And guess what? I didn't laugh. Not once."

"Laugh about what?" asked Charlie, butting in like always.

Dyamonde put her hands on

her hips. "Our conversation has abso-tively, posi-lutely nothing to do with you, Charlie."

"Huh?"

Damaris did that funny thing with her face again. She smiled.

The Three Musketeers

When Free came back to school the next day, he found himself part of a trio. He didn't get to vote on it, but that was okay. He liked Damaris. She seemed to be smart like Dyamonde. Plus, she was almost as tall as he was.

Dyamonde didn't mind being the short one. She made up for

it by having the biggest mouth. When it came to talking, nobody could beat her!

The three friends sat together at lunch, did homework together, picked each other for games and made trips to the library together. They visited each other at home too. Except they never went to the shelter with Damaris. There wasn't any space for visitors there, plus Damaris never invited them.

Free didn't know anything about Damaris living in the shelter, so he wondered why she never invited them home. Which is why, one day at the library, he leaned across the table and asked, "Damaris, how come you never invite us to your house? You ashamed of us or something?"

Damaris jumped back, stinging from Free's question. It was too close to the truth. She *was* ashamed of something: where she lived. Dyamonde was mad at Free for bringing it up.

She kicked him under the table. Hard.

"Ouch!" said Free. "Whaddya do that for? I was just joking."

"Shhhh!" said Dyamonde in a

67

loud whisper. "We're in the library, and we have to be quiet. Don't you know anything?"

Free was confused. They'd talked in the library lots of times. He was about to say that, but Dyamonde gave him her don't-you-even-think-about-it look, so he kept his mouth shut.

When Free was done with his book report, he headed home and left the girls to themselves. Which was perfect. Dyamonde had a private invitation just for Damaris.

"Hey, you want to spend the

night at my house on Friday? On Saturday mornings, my mom makes the yummiest pancakes on the planet."

"Fantasmic!" said Damaris. "I'll ask my mom."

Sleepover

Dyamonde woke up happy the next Saturday. She hadn't had a friend spend the night since she left Brooklyn.

Damaris seemed to have a good time too, at first. She liked helping Dyamonde set the table. She laughed when Dyamonde made gagging sounds the minute

Mrs. Daniel spooned brussels sprouts on their plates. She liked playing Monopoly. She really liked joining Dyamonde against Mrs. Daniel in a game of gin rummy, especially when they won and got extra ice cream for dessert. But the next morning, Damaris seemed sad. Dyamonde noticed it over breakfast.

"Are your pancakes okay?" asked Dyamonde. Damaris nodded yes.

"What's wrong, then?" asked Dyamonde.

Damaris shrugged. She poured

more syrup on her pancakes and diced them into tiny pieces before finally putting one in her mouth. Dyamonde always did that when she wanted to make food last longer.

Is that what she's doing? wondered Dyamonde.

"My mom can make lots more pancakes if you want," said Dyamonde.

Damaris nodded and kept chewing slower than slow.

"Aren't these pancakes the best?" asked Dyamonde.

"Honey," said Mrs. Daniel,

"leave the child alone and let her eat in peace."

Dyamonde sighed and went back to working on her own stack of blueberry pancake heaven. She was licking her fingers when Damaris said, "I wish—I wish I could stay here. I wish I didn't have to go back to that shelter."

That's why she's sad, thought Dyamonde.

A tear slid down the girl's cheek. Dyamonde ran over to her friend and hugged her so tight, Damaris felt like the middle of a love sandwich.

"Come here, honey," said Mrs. Daniel, prying Damaris loose. "Let's get that face of yours cleaned up."

While Mrs. Daniel led Damaris to the bathroom, Dyamonde cleared the table and washed the breakfast dishes. In a few minutes, Damaris was at the door, face scrubbed, ready to say good-bye.

"Wait up," said Dyamonde. "I'll walk you."

Honey, I Love

Dyamonde left Damaris at the entrance to the shelter and said a quick good-bye. She was feeling as sad as her friend now. What made her especially sad was that she couldn't give her friend a new place to live. She couldn't give her back all her clothes and toys. Even so, Dyamonde kept thinking, *There must be something I can do.*

Dyamonde walked past Second Time Around and spotted something in the store's window.

"That's it!" said Dyamonde.

She doubled back to the entrance, ducked inside and headed straight for the book aisle.

Dyamonde started looking.

Biographies. Fairy Tales. Science Fiction.

"There!" said Dyamonde.

Poetry.

Dyamonde flipped through

several titles until she found one she liked.

"Perfect!" said Dyamonde.

"Hello there," said the cash register lady. "Haven't seen you in a while. What have you got there?"

"Poetry," said Dyamonde.

"Well, that's a first. I don't think I've ever seen you buy a book here before."

"It's for my friend," said Dyamonde.

"Oh! Well, I hope she likes it."

"Me too," said Dyamonde. "Me too."

• • •

The following Monday, Dyamonde got to school early. She wrote a note, slipped it inside the poetry book and left both on the chair where Damaris sat. That way, she'd be sure to see the book, first thing.

As the class filled up, Dyamonde kept her eye on the book to make sure no one else took it by mistake. Once Damaris got to her seat and found the book, Dyamonde relaxed. But only a little. She was still nervous about the choice, seeing as how poetry was not her thing, and she didn't know if Damaris would think the book was any good.

What if she doesn't like it? thought Dyamonde. *What if I picked the wrong one?* She should like the title, though.

The book was called *Honey, I Love,* by Eloise Greenfield. Dyamonde remembered Mrs. Cordell saying this author was really special.

Dyamonde crossed her fingers and watched Damaris scan a few pages of the book. Dyamonde held her breath until Damaris looked her way. She was smiling.

Then she read Dyamonde's note and smiled even more.

Good luck with your poem writing.

I hope this helps.

Dyamonde

After class, Damaris rushed up to Dyamonde.

"How did you know?" she asked, her eyes gleaming.

"How did I know what?" asked Dyamonde.

"That Eloise Greenfield is my favorite poet!"

Dyamonde felt all tingly. "She is?"

Damaris nodded so hard, Dyamonde thought her head would fall off.

"Wow," said Dyamonde, speechless for once.

"Before we lost our house, I had copies of every single book she ever wrote," said Damaris. "But now . . ."

Dyamonde noticed a sudden sadness pulling down the corners of her friend's mouth.

"I know what," said Dyamonde, thinking quickly. "One Saturday, you can join me and Free when we go treasure hunting. Maybe we can find another Eloise Greenfield book for not too much money in the same place where I found this one."

Damaris managed to smile again.

"Yeah?"

"Why not?" said Dyamonde. "But right now, we better get some lunch, 'cause I'm about to chew off my own arm, I'm so hungry."

Damaris slipped her new "old" copy of *Honey, I Love* into her backpack and followed the amazing Dyamonde Daniel out of the room.

And the Winner Is

Dyamonde opened the news-paper to the Kids' Page.

Oh, geez, thought Dyamonde. *I'll never hear the end of it.*

Free's poem made it to the Sunday paper. He chose to write about nature. Sort of. His poem was titled "Give a Pigeon a Break." Dyamonde read the title and laughed out loud. Then she noticed the poem at the top of the page, written by Damaris. It had won first prize! And why wouldn't it? After all, Damaris had taken Dyamonde's wonderful advice to write about home. Dyamonde could barely stop patting herself on the back long enough to cut out the poem and tape it to the fridge. She was thrilled for Damaris.

Rich
by Damaris Dancer

Home is a word
I forgot how to spell.
I live in a shelter,
but I never tell.

The place is all right,
but it makes me sad.
I remember our old house,
the great toys we had,

the bed where I slept
all by myself,
the rows of books
that crowded our shelf.

But Mom lost her job
and we had to move.
Now I always feel
I have something to prove.

Well, I may seem poor,
with no home of my own,
but I'm rich in good friends,
so I'm never alone.

Dyamonde hadn't even entered the contest, but in a way, she felt like a winner. She'd learned to like poetry, thanks to Damaris. Which is what she told her the next day at lunch when she could get a word in edgewise.

"I'm a published poet now," said Free.

"Yes. We know," said Dyamonde.

"It's like I told you, I'm a poet and I know it."

"And now so do the rest of us," said Dyamonde.

"Abso-tively, posi-lutely," said Damaris.

Free shook his head. He always tuned out whenever Damaris started speaking in made-up words.

"Look," said Free, "I'm just sayin' I got skills."

Dyamonde sighed. *I knew I was*

never going to hear the end of this, she thought.

"You're right, Free. You've got skills. But Damaris has even more 'skills,' which is why she won the contest. Your poem was the best," said Dyamonde, trying to turn the attention to Damaris.

Free shrugged. "Your poem was righteous, I give you that," said Free.

"Well, I don't know about *righteous,*" said Damaris, "but it's the truth. And my mom told me you should never be ashamed of the truth."

"Word," said Free, silent for half a second. Then he tapped his poem in the Sunday newspaper, saying, "But look at this baby. It's beautiful! Come on, be honest. Y'all both know that Fabulous Free should have been the winner!"

Free struck a pose like he was waiting for some reporter to run up and snap his picture.

"Oh, *puleeze!*" said Dyamonde. She and Damaris burst out laughing. Before Free knew it, he was laughing too.

Born and raised in New York City, **Nikki Grimes** began composing verse at the age of six and has been writing ever since. She is the critically acclaimed author of numerous award-winning books for children and young adults, including Coretta Scott King Award winner *Bronx Masquerade*, Coretta Scott King Honor winner *The Road to Paris* and *New York Times* bestseller *Barack Obama: Son of Promise, Child of Hope* (illustrated by Bryan Collier). In addition to a Coretta Scott King Award and four Coretta Scott King Honors, her work has received accolades such as the NCTE Award for Excellence in Poetry for Children, *Booklist* Editors' Choice, ALA Notable, Bank Street College Book of the Year, *Horn Book* Fanfare, *American Bookseller* Pick of the List, Notable Social Studies Trade Book, NAACP Image Award Finalist, and the Golden Dolphin Award, an award given by the Southern California Children's Booksellers Association in recognition of an author's body of work. She lives in Corona, California.

Visit her at www.nikkigrimes.com.